Topsy +

CW00456684

have their hair cut

Jean and Gareth Adamson

Blackie

Copyright © 1989 Jean and Gareth Adamson
First published in 1989 by Blackie and Son Limited
Reprinted 1991

British Library Cataloguing in Publication Data
Adamson, Jean, 1928—
Topsy and Tim have their hair cut
I. Title   II. Adamson, Gareth, 1925–1982
823′.914[J]

ISBN 0-216-92597-5
ISBN 0-216-92596-7 Pbk

Blackie and Son Limited
7 Leicester Place
London WC2H 7BP

Printed in Portugal

One Saturday morning, Mummy went to get her hair cut. Topsy and Tim stayed at home to help Dad mend the kitchen tap.

Mending the tap was a difficult job.
Dad got a bit cross. Topsy and Tim
wished they'd gone to the hairdresser
with Mummy.
'May we play hairdressers, Dad?'
asked Topsy.
'Yes,' said Dad. 'Bother this spanner.'

There was a big mirror in Mummy
and Dad's bedroom. Topsy went
to get her play scissors and Tim
found a comb. Topsy cut Tim's hair.
Tim cut Topsy's hair. It was
hard work because the play scissors
were not sharp.

'We don't look like us any more,
said Topsy.
'That mirror must be wrong,' said Tim.

When Mummy came home she was
very cross with them.
'Topsy and Tim, what have you done!'
she said. 'You know you shouldn't play
with scissors. You could have hurt
yourselves.' Then she laughed.
'Just look at you!' she said.

Mummy took Topsy and Tim
straight to the hairdresser.
'They can't put your hair back,'
she said, 'but they can make
what is left look tidy.'
Topsy and Tim hoped none of
their friends would see them.

Topsy and Tim had never been
to a hairdresser before.
Mummy had always cut their hair.
'You first, Tim,' said Mummy.
Pauline, the hairdresser, held out
a waterproof cape for him.
Tim wouldn't let her put it on.

'I'll go first,' said Topsy. Pauline put
the cape on her and took her to sit
at a special hairwashing basin.
'Put your head right back, Topsy,'
said Pauline. 'Then I can wash
your hair.'

Topsy enjoyed having her hair washed.
Tim came to watch.
'Can I have mine done now?' he asked.

Pauline showed Topsy and Tim how
their chairs went up and down.
Then she began to cut Topsy's hair.
'That looks nice,' said Mummy.

Then it was Tim's turn. 'Shall I give you a crew-cut, Tim?' asked Pauline.
'Why not?' said Mummy.

Pauline dried Topsy's hair with
a blow-dryer. Topsy liked the feeling
of warm air on her head.
Tim's hair was so short it had dried
by itself.

Pauline held up a mirror
so that Topsy and Tim
could see their new
haircuts.
'We still don't look like us,'
said Topsy.
'But we do look nice,'
said Tim.
'Next time you want
a haircut, let Pauline
do it,' said Mummy.

When Topsy and Tim got home,
Dad pretended he didn't know them.
'It's us, Dad!' they said.

'You do look good,' said Dad.
'Perhaps I should have my hair
cut too.'

Topsy and Tim's hair took a long time
to grow again, but it did at last.
Here they are, to prove it.